Sophomore Shenanigans

Jariv - Reuel Josh V. Anda

Ukiyoto Publishing

All global publishing rights are held by

Ukiyoto Publishing

Published in 2024

Content Copyright © Jariv - Reuel Josh V. Anda

ISBN 9789367953051

All rights reserved.
No part of this publication may be reproduced, transmitted, or stored in a retrieval system, in any form by any means, electronic, mechanical, photocopying, recording or otherwise, without the prior permission of the publisher.

The moral rights of the author have been asserted.

This is a work of fiction. Names, characters, businesses, places, events, locales, and incidents are either the products of the author's imagination or used in a fictitious manner. Any resemblance to actual persons, living or dead, or actual events is purely coincidental.

This book is sold subject to the condition that it shall not by way of trade or otherwise, be lent, resold, hired out or otherwise circulated, without the publisher's prior consent, in any form of binding or cover other than that in which it is published.

www.ukiyoto.com

I dedicated this book for those who take a lot pressure from families and also from everyone.

I also dedicated this book for my Mama and Papa and for my John A. Anda's Family.

I also want to thank my cousin Maryjade Anne who also an author at Ukiyoto, who inspired me to write and publish book.

Contents

Intro: 1
Chapter 1: Bagong Simula 2
Chapter 2: Physics Class 6
Chapter 3: Presentation Day 15
Chapter 4: The Sophomore Challenge 19
Chapter 5: Aftermath 24
Chapter 6: A New Rival 27
Chapter 7: Clash of the Minds 31
Chapter 8: The Final Showdown 35
Chapter 9: Crossroads of the Heart 42
Chapter 10: Twists of Fate 46
About the Author 53

Intro:

"**B**akit parang ang hirap ng lahat?" I whispered to myself as I watched my classmates rush through the busy halls of San Ignacio High. Ang daming tawanan, pero sa loob ko, parang may nag-aalburuto. "This year was supposed to be fun, pero bakit ang dami kong iniisip?"

I tightened my grip on my backpack, feeling the pressure of everyone's expectations. Isa akong sophomore, pero parang ang dami ko nang problema. I glanced at the cafeteria, filled with noise and laughter, but it all felt distant. "Kailangan kong magpakatatag," I told myself. "Kasi sa likod ng mga ngiti, may mga lihim na hindi ko alam kung kakayanin ko."

Taking a deep breath, I stepped into the crowd, ready to face another day of confusion and secrets. Because in high school, trusting someone is the biggest challenge of all.

Chapter 1: Bagong Simula

Vacation is almost over, and I know I need to start focusing on my studies. I spent most of the break tutoring, kasi sabi ng parents ko kailangan daw. I didn't really expect them to make me do that, pero okay lang. Another year, another new school—again! This time, they've enrolled me at San Ignacio High School. It's a private school, and based on my past experiences, mataas lagi ang expectations kapag private school. Lalo na't ako ay anak ng mga Astorga.

I'm both excited and nervous. New school means new friends, new teachers, and new challenges. Pero hindi rin madali kasi every time I get used to a place, we move again. My parents say it's for the best, pero minsan nakakainis na rin. My mom is a doctor at Saint Merced Private Hospital, and my dad's an attorney. Since I'm an only child, they put a lot of pressure on me. Gusto nilang maging engineer ako someday, kaya kailangan daw mag-focus sa studies.

"My name is Javriel Astorga, I'm 16 years old, and I believe that if you want to get high grades, you need to study." I introduced myself in front of the class, feeling a bit nervous pero hindi na katulad ng dati. Sanay na rin kasi ako magpakilala in front of new faces, kasi nga lagi akong bago sa mga schools.

After introducing myself, I quickly sat down next to a girl wearing hoodie with thick glasses, messy hair, and a lot of pimples. Tahimik siya, so I didn't say anything either. While listening to the other introductions, someone suddenly tapped my shoulder.

"Hey, Jariv—"

"Javriel, my name is Javriel," I corrected him politely with a shy smile.

"Oh, sorry! 'di ako magaling when talking about memorizing names, haha. By the way, I'm Gabby, short for Gabriel," he said with a big smile.

"Hi, nice to meet you, Gabriel!" I replied, trying to be friendly.

"Since you know my name, can I borrow one of your extra pens? Kanina ko pa napansin, ang dami mong ballpen, parang ikaw may-ari ng bookstore, haha!" he joked while chuckling.

"Actually, my aunt owns a bookstore," I replied, laughing a little. "Of course, you can borrow one. Keep it, though."

"Wow, thanks, Javriel! By the way, this is Mia, my best friend since kindergarten. Mabait 'yan, at matalino pa," he said while introducing the girl sitting next to me—yung girl with thick glasses.

"Hi Mia, I'm Javriel," I greeted her, extending my hand.

"Hi Javriel, nice to meet you," she said, shaking my hand with a shy smile.

As we talked, I realized we had some things in common. Pareho kaming mahilig mag-aral, and mahilig sa physics, pero may isang bagay na iba. Mia's a scholar, so hindi sila kasing yaman ng pamilya namin. Hindi siya nakakasali sa iba't-ibang activities sa school kasi medyo mahal ang ibang events. But still, I could tell she was smart and kind.

After all the introductions were done, our teacher, Mrs. Santiago, introduced herself. She started explaining the grading system for Physics. Mukhang strict siya, pero mukhang fair din naman.

"Class dismissed!" Mrs. Santiago said after explaining everything.

I packed up my stuff, ready to leave. As I stood up, Gabby called out to me again.

"Hey, Javriel! Sama ka sa amin ni Mia sa cafeteria. Masarap daw food dun, sabi ng mga seniors."

"Sure, game ako. Saan ba 'yun?" I asked, feeling a bit excited to explore the school with them.

"Medyo Exiting to for sure!" my thoughts.

As we walked down the hallways, I couldn't help but feel a mix of excitement and curiosity. Malaki 'tong school, and there were so many students. Pero okay lang, at least I already made new friends. Maybe this year wouldn't be so bad after all.

Pagdating namin sa cafeteria, ang daming tao. Students from different year levels were sitting at the tables, eating and chatting. It felt lively and chaotic at the same time. Some students were singing, and doing TikTok. Gabby led us to an empty table near the window.

"Okay lang ba dito tayo? Parang dito tambayan ng mga upperclassmen," I asked, feeling a bit unsure.

"Okay lang yan. Hindi naman sila nagmamaldita, promise," Sabi ni Mia, sitting down with her tray.

"First day pa lang, dami ko nang naririnig na kwento about San Ignacio. May mga strict na teachers daw, tapos may mga activities na sobrang hirap. Sabi nga ng kuya ko, dapat daw maghanda ako sa 'Sophomore Challenge'," Gabby said, taking a bite of his sandwich.

"Sophomore Challenge?" I asked, curious. "Ano yun?"

"It's this big event for sophomores. Parang survival test, sabi nila. Hindi ko pa sure yung ibang details, pero mukhang intense," he explained.

"Hala, parang scary, if ever na gagawin na natin yun I hope na, maka-survive ako." Mia commented, looking a bit worried.

"Nako, kaya natin yan!" I said, trying to lighten the mood. "Sanay naman tayo sa mga challenges, diba?"

As we continued talking, I felt a bit more at ease. Hindi ko man kilala lahat dito, but at least I wasn't alone. Maybe this year, at San Ignacio, would be the start of something good.

Chapter 2: Physics Class

"Alright, class, ang magiging partners niyo for this project ay naka-assign na," Mrs. Santiago announced as she began reading the names from her list.

I leaned back in my chair, feeling confident. Physics was one of my favorite subjects, kaya I was pretty excited about the project. Nang marinig ko ang pangalan ko, I sat up straight.

"Ms. Santa Rosario, I'm pairing you with Mr. Astorga."

Napatingin ako kay Mia, who sat a few chairs away, her messy hair partially covering her face. Nagtaas siya ng tingin at ngumiti nang kaunti, pero halata ang kaba.

"This is great, Mia! Kayang-kaya natin 'to," I said, smiling at her.

Mia pushed her glasses up and gave a small nod. "Oo nga, pero…" She glanced over at Gabby, who was sitting at the back, looking bored. "Si Gabby? Wala siyang partner."

"Don't worry, kaya ni Gabby yun. Andito lang tayo if he needs help," I reassured her.

Mrs. Santiago clapped her hands to get everyone's attention. "I expect nothing but excellence in this project. Quantum Mechanics ang topic, and I know it's a challenging subject. But I believe in you all. Now, head to the library to start your research."

Sa library, ang daming estudyante na naghanap ng books at references. The space smelled of old paper and coffee, and it had this calming atmosphere that made me want to stay longer. Mia and I found a quiet spot near the physics section.

"Okay, simulan na natin," Mia said, pulling out her notebook.

I scanned the shelves, looking for anything that mentioned Quantum Mechanics. Then, something caught my attention—a thick, old album tucked in between the books. Out of curiosity, kinuha ko ito at binuksan. The first few pages were filled with black-and-white photos of students. As I flipped further, a photo stopped me in my tracks.

"Mia, tingnan mo 'to," I called her over.

She leaned closer. "Wait... sila ba 'yan? Parents mo?"

I nodded slowly, my eyes fixed on the photo. My mom was smiling, holding up a certificate, while my dad stood beside her, looking proud. On the next page, there was another photo of them working on a project. At ang topic? Quantum Mechanics din.

"No way! Javriel, ang cool nito. Maybe we can ask your parents for tips. Sobrang helpful siguro ng mga ginawa nila dati!" Mia said, her voice filled with excitement.

I hesitated. "Alam mo naman ang mga magulang ko, laging busy. Pero... siguro pwede ko silang tanungin mamaya."

"Yes! Try mo lang. I'm sure they'll want to help."

We continued our search, flipping through books and writing down notes. Ang dami naming nakitang ideas about Quantum Mechanics, and we were already brainstorming how to present it.

"Galing! Ang dami nating nahanap," Mia said, her energy contagious.

I smiled back. "Oo nga eh. I think we're off to a good start."

Habang nagre-research, I couldn't help but glance at the album again. Seeing my parents in those photos felt strange—parang may koneksyon ako sa kanila na hindi ko usually nararamdaman. Maybe this project wasn't just about Physics—it could also be a way to understand them better.

Nang matapos na ang research namin, nag-decide kami ni Mia to organize our notes.

"Bukas, we can start drafting our outline," she said habang nililigpit ang mga libro.

"Sounds good," I replied. Then I paused. "Pero Mia, paano kaya kung hindi available ang parents ko? Paano natin maa-achieve yung level ng project nila?"

Mia adjusted her glasses and gave me a determined look. "Alam mo, kahit hindi sila makatulong, kaya natin 'to. Pero kung may time sila, mas maganda. Let's just do our best, okay?"

Her words gave me confidence. "Tama ka. Kaya natin 'to."

Pag-uwi ko sa bahay, I found my mom in her study, typing away on her laptop. My dad was on the phone, pacing in the living room. Busy as usual. I decided to wait until dinner to bring it up.

During dinner, habang kumakain kami ng roast chicken, I finally gathered the courage to ask.

"Mom, Dad, may project kami about Quantum Mechanics," I started, keeping my tone casual. "I found an old class photo sa library kanina. You guys did the same topic, right?"

My mom paused mid-bite, looking surprised. "You found that? Wow, that was a long time ago."

My dad chuckled. "Quantum Mechanics... that was a tough one. Pero we enjoyed it."

"Pwede ba kaming humingi ng tips?" I asked hesitantly.

My mom smiled. "Of course, Javriel. Pero you'll have to do most of the work, ha? We'll just guide you."

I nodded eagerly. "Thank you, Mom! Thank you, Dad!"

The next day at school, I told Mia about it.

"They said yes!" I told her, unable to hide my excitement.

"Talaga? Ang saya! This is going to be awesome!" Mia said, clapping her hands.

Gabby walked up to us, holding his tray of snacks. "Ano'ng awesome?"

"Physics project namin," Mia replied.

Gabby groaned. "Good luck sa inyo. Ako, wala pa ring partner."

"Eh di sali ka sa amin," I joked.

He laughed. "Pass na muna. Pero good luck talaga, ha?"

As Mia and I continued planning, I felt a sense of excitement I hadn't felt in a long time. This wasn't just about acing a project—it felt like a chance to connect with my parents, to make new friends, and to discover what I was capable of.

San Ignacio High was starting to feel like home.

The days flew by, and Mia and I were busy with the project. Ang dami naming kailangan pag-usapan—our hypothesis, experiment design, and even the materials we would use. Luckily, San Ignacio's library had most of what we needed. Mia was incredibly focused, always scribbling down notes or sketching diagrams.

"Mia, masyado mo nang sineryoso, baka sumabog 'yang utak mo," I joked one afternoon habang nagme-meeting kami sa cafeteria.

"Excuse me, Mr. Astorga," she replied, raising an eyebrow. "This is how scholars work. Pero ikaw, mukhang chill na chill ka lang."

I laughed. "Hindi naman. I'm just good at pretending hindi ako kinakabahan."

She shook her head and chuckled. "Let's just finish this part before Gabby shows up and distracts us."

Almost on cue, Gabby appeared with his tray of food. "Guys! Kumusta na ang future scientists?"

"Eto, alive pa naman," I answered, gesturing to our pile of books and notes.

Gabby smirked. "Good for you. Ako, hanggang ngayon, iniisip pa rin kung anong gagawin sa project."

"Tama si Mia, kaya mo yan, Gab. Huwag kang masyadong chill," I teased.

By the end of the week, I decided to finally sit down with my mom and dad to ask for advice. Sunday afternoon, I found them relaxing in the living room.

"Mom, Dad, can I show you what we've done so far?" I asked, holding a folder with our notes and diagrams.

My mom patted the seat beside her. "Of course, Javriel. Let's see."

I explained our plan, starting with the basics of Quantum Mechanics and the experiment we wanted to try. My dad listened intently, nodding every now and then.

"Your approach is solid," he said after I finished. "Pero may isa kayong dapat tandaan: in projects like this, it's not just about the final product. It's about the process. Focus on learning as you go."

My mom added, "And don't overcomplicate things. Keep your experiment clear and simple. Sometimes, less is more."

Their advice made so much sense, and I couldn't wait to share it with Mia.

The next day, I told Mia everything my parents had said.

"Ang galing!" she exclaimed. "We can definitely simplify some parts para mas smooth ang presentation natin."

We spent the afternoon fine-tuning our outline and making our experiment more realistic. Mia was good at breaking down complex ideas, habang ako naman ang taga-organize ng mga gagawin. We were a good team.

A few days later, we were finally ready to test our experiment. The school's physics lab was like something out of a sci-fi movie—may mga equipment na parang hindi pa namin nakikita sa buong buhay namin.

"Okay, moment of truth," Mia said as she carefully adjusted the setup.

I nodded, trying to hide my nervousness. "Sana gumana 'to."

As we ran the simulation, we watched the numbers and graphs appear on the screen. It wasn't perfect, pero it was working.

"Javriel, it's working!" Mia said excitedly, her eyes lighting up behind her glasses.

I grinned. "Told you, kaya natin 'to."

Later that day, habang nasa rooftop kami to relax after our lab session, Mia suddenly asked, "Javriel, may gusto ka bang patunayan sa project na 'to?"

I paused, surprised by her question. "Bakit mo natanong?"

"Parang kasi sobrang determined mo, and you keep talking about your parents. Gusto mo bang ipakita sa kanila na kaya mo rin?"

Napatingin ako sa langit, thinking. "Maybe. Parang ganun na nga. I mean, they're always busy, pero gusto ko rin naman na maging proud sila sa akin. Ikaw, Mia? Bakit ka sobrang sipag?"

She shrugged, looking down at her hands. "Scholar ako, Javriel. Kung hindi ako magtrabaho nang mabuti, baka mawala 'yung scholarship ko. I don't have the luxury to fail."

"Pero ang galing mo, Mia. Kahit sobrang daming expectations, you still manage to do great," I said sincerely.

"Thanks," she said softly, a small smile forming on her lips.

As the days passed, Mia and I worked harder, and we became closer friends. Gabby continued to be our comic relief, dropping by to make us laugh whenever things got too stressful.

When the day of the project presentation finally arrived, I felt a mix of excitement and nervousness. Pero isang bagay ang sure ako—this project wasn't just about Quantum Mechanics anymore. It was about proving to myself that I could handle challenges, making my parents proud, and appreciating the people around me who believed in me.

Chapter 3: Presentation Day

The long-awaited day had finally come. Sa araw na ito, lahat ng projects sa Physics class ni Mrs. Santiago ay ipapakita. The tension in the room was almost palpable as everyone hurried to set up their materials. Kahit ang mga usually chill na students looked stressed.

"Relax, Javriel," Mia whispered beside me as we arranged our presentation board and experiment setup. "We've prepared for this. Kaya natin 'to."

I nodded, though I couldn't hide the nervous energy running through me. Gabby passed by and gave me a thumbs-up. "Good luck, future Einstein!"

"Thanks, Gab!" I replied with a grin, kahit nanginginig na ang mga kamay ko.

Mrs. Santiago stood at the front of the classroom and clapped her hands to get everyone's attention. "Alright, class. Let's begin. Remember, this isn't just about the experiment—it's also about how well you can explain the concepts behind it. Let's start with... Mr. Astorga and Ms. Santa Rosario."

Napalingon ako kay Mia, who adjusted her glasses and gave me a firm nod. "Let's do this."

As we stood in front of the class, I took a deep breath and started the presentation.

"Good morning, everyone. Our project is about Quantum Mechanics, a complex but fascinating topic that explores the behavior of matter and energy on the atomic and subatomic levels," I began, trying to keep my voice steady.

Mia took over, explaining the basic principles of quantum entanglement and how it applied to our experiment. She spoke confidently, her passion for the subject shining through.

"We created a simulation to demonstrate how particles behave in a quantum state," she said, pointing to the screen where our data was displayed.

When it was my turn, I explained the experiment setup and the results we obtained. Every time I felt nervous, I would glance at Mia, who always gave me an encouraging smile.

Finally, we demonstrated the simulation. The class watched intently as the graphs and data updated in real time.

"Wow," someone whispered from the back.

"That's so cool," another classmate added.

Mrs. Santiago nodded approvingly. "Very impressive. You both clearly understand the topic, and your experiment was well-executed. Great job."

Hearing those words felt like a weight had been lifted off my shoulders. Mia and I exchanged triumphant smiles as we returned to our seats.

During the break, Gabby rushed over to us.

"Grabe, guys! That was amazing! Parang nasa science fair sa college level!" he said, his hands flailing in excitement.

"Thanks, Gab. Pero teamwork talaga," Mia replied, still looking a bit flushed from the adrenaline.

"Teamwork? More like genius-level brains," Gabby teased, making us laugh.

Later that day, habang nasa cafeteria kami, I couldn't help but reflect on everything that had happened.

"Javriel, mukhang may gusto kang sabihin," Mia said, sipping her iced tea.

I looked at her and Gabby, who were both staring at me expectantly. "Oo, meron nga. Thank you, Mia. Hindi ko magagawa 'tong project na 'to without you. You pushed me to do my best."

She blushed slightly and adjusted her glasses. "Grabe ka naman. Team effort nga, diba?"

"And Gabby," I added, turning to him. "Thanks for making us laugh when we needed it the most."

"Wala 'yon. Basta libre mo ako ng fries next time," he joked, making all of us laugh again.

That evening, when I got home, my mom and dad were waiting for me in the living room.

"How was the presentation?" my mom asked, her eyes full of curiosity.

"It went great! Mrs. Santiago said we did a good job," I replied, feeling proud.

My dad nodded approvingly. "I'm glad to hear that. Hard work always pays off, doesn't it?"

"Yeah," I said, realizing how true that was.

As I headed to my room, I felt a sense of accomplishment I hadn't felt in a long time. This project wasn't just about grades—it was about proving to myself that I could rise to the challenge, no matter how tough things got.

San Ignacio High still had its mysteries and challenges, but for the first time, I felt like I belonged. And that feeling? That was worth everything.

Chapter 4: The Sophomore Challenge

"Alright, class! I have an exciting announcement," Mrs. Santiago said with a wide grin as she walked into the room. "The Sophomore Challenge is officially happening next month. I suggest you start preparing now."

Nagkatinginan kaming lahat sa klase. Parang nabuhusan ng malamig na tubig ang buong room.

"The Sophomore Challenge?" I whispered to Mia, who was already flipping through her notebook.

"Yes, I heard about it last year," she replied. "It's a school-wide event for second-year students. Parang Amazing Race meets survival camp daw."

Gabby, who was sitting behind us, leaned forward. "May kuya ako na sumali noon. Sabi niya, sobrang intense daw. May physical challenges, academic puzzles, at teamwork tests."

I groaned. "Great. As if Physics wasn't stressful enough."

During lunch, we couldn't stop talking about the challenge.

"Parang exciting din naman," Mia said, nibbling on her sandwich. "It's a chance to prove ourselves."

Gabby chuckled. "Easy for you to say. Scholar ka, kaya mong sagutin lahat ng academic puzzles. Paano naman kami ni Javriel? Physical lang ata ang laban namin."

I smirked. "Uy, underestimate mo naman kami. Baka naman may itatagal din kami sa academics, Gab."

"Okay, fine," Gabby said, raising his hands in surrender. "Pero sana hindi ganun kahirap. Hindi ako pwede masaktan, mukha ko ang puhunan."

We all burst out laughing, the tension from earlier finally easing a bit.

The days leading up to the event were filled with preparation. Each section was required to form groups of five. It wasn't hard for me to decide on my team—Mia and Gabby were obvious choices. Dalawa pang classmates namin, si Lex at Carina, joined in.

Lex was athletic, a varsity player sa basketball team. Meanwhile, Carina was a math whiz but had a feisty personality na minsan nakakainis, minsan nakakatawa.

"Kaya ba natin 'to?" Lex asked during one of our strategy meetings.

"Kaya, basta magtulungan tayo," Mia said confidently.

"Agree. Kailangan natin i-balance ang strengths natin," Carina added, flipping her pen.

Gabby grinned. "So, ako ang magiging taga-boost ng morale. Simple lang ang role ko—maging comedian ng group."

"Baka distraction, hindi morale," I teased, earning a laugh from everyone.

On the day of the challenge, the school grounds transformed into a massive game arena. Flags, obstacle courses, and stations were set up all over the campus. The energy was electric—students from all sophomore sections were buzzing with excitement and nerves.

"Alright, team!" I said, trying to pump everyone up. "Focus lang tayo. We've got this."

"Sure ka?" Gabby teased, patting my shoulder. "Mukha kang mas kinakabahan pa sa amin."

"Hindi naman obvious, Gab," Carina said sarcastically, rolling her eyes.

Mia adjusted her glasses and gave me a reassuring smile. "We'll be fine, Jav. Let's just take it one challenge at a time."

The first task was an academic puzzle. May mga riddles na kailangan naming i-solve using logic and a bit of creativity. Mia and Carina dominated this round, their brains working in sync like a well-oiled machine.

"Done!" Mia exclaimed, raising her hand.

The facilitator checked our answers and nodded. "Correct. You may proceed to the next station."

"Wow, ang bibilis niyo!" Lex said, clearly impressed.

The second task was a physical obstacle course. Dito pumasok ang skills ni Lex and, surprisingly, Gabby.

"Ang bilis mo pala tumakbo, Gab!" I shouted as we all climbed over a tall wall.

"Secret lang 'yan, bro! Hindi ko lang pinapakita na athletic din ako," he replied, panting but smiling.

The third task was a teamwork challenge. Kailangan naming magtawid ng mga gamit gamit ang rope bridge without dropping anything. This was the hardest part so far.

"Mia, steady lang," I said as she carefully passed a box to Gabby.

"Ang hirap nito," she muttered, her hands trembling slightly.

"We're almost there," Carina said, guiding Lex across the bridge.

It took us longer than we expected, but we finally made it.

As we reached the final station, pagod na kami lahat, but the adrenaline kept us going. The last task was a trivia challenge that tested everything—from general knowledge to school history.

"Mia, ikaw na bahala dito," Gabby said, leaning against the table.

"Hindi puwede. Team effort dapat," Mia replied.

We huddled together, combining our knowledge to answer each question. Every time we got one right, the excitement grew.

Finally, we completed the challenge. Exhausted but exhilarated, our team cheered as we crossed the finish line.

"We did it!" I shouted, high-fiving everyone.

"Grabe, ang hirap, pero ang saya!" Gabby exclaimed, slumping onto the grass.

Mia adjusted her glasses and smiled. "Told you, teamwork lang ang kailangan."

"Fine, Mia, ikaw na ang MVP," Carina said, laughing.

As we sat there catching our breath, I realized something. This wasn't just about winning or losing—it was about discovering how far we could go when we worked together.

Chapter 5: Aftermath

The day after the Sophomore Challenge felt like a blur. Everyone in school was still buzzing about the event. Sa cafeteria, halos lahat ng naririnig ko ay kwento tungkol sa iba't ibang teams. Sino raw ang mabilis, sino ang nadapa, at sino ang muntik nang sumuko.

"Uy, Jav, ang dami kong naririnig na comments tungkol sa team natin," Gabby said as he plopped his tray beside me. "Sikat na sikat ka daw kasi parang captain ng group!"

"Captain? Ako? Hindi naman," I said, shaking my head.

"Eh ikaw 'yung nag-lead, kaya natural lang 'yon," Mia chimed in as she adjusted her glasses. "But to be fair, team effort talaga 'yung ginawa natin."

Lex joined us, carrying his basketball. "Sabi ng mga ka-varsity ko, ang galing daw ng team natin. Eh ako nga, muntik nang malaglag sa rope bridge."

"Haha, oo nga, Lex! Akala ko babagsak ka na nun," Carina teased as she sat down with her tray.

"You're one to talk! Sino 'yung muntik mahulog kasi na-sobrang gigil magbigay ng box?" Lex shot back, making everyone laugh.

Later that day, Mrs. Santiago entered the classroom with a proud smile on her face.

"Class, I just want to congratulate everyone for participating in the Sophomore Challenge. You all did amazing work. It's not just about the tasks but how you handled the pressure and worked as a team. And I'm happy to announce..." She paused, building suspense.

"...that Team Astorga placed third overall!"

The entire class erupted in cheers and applause. Mia's face lit up, and Gabby nearly fell out of his chair from excitement.

"Third place? Hindi na masama!" Lex said, clapping his hands.

"Congrats, everyone!" Carina added with a wide smile.

"Let's give them a big round of applause," Mrs. Santiago said, leading the entire class in a round of claps.

After class, as we walked out of the room, Gabby turned to us with a mischievous grin.

"So, dahil nanalo tayo, libre mo na kami, Jav."

"What? Bakit ako? Team effort nga, diba?" I protested, laughing.

"Dahil ikaw ang captain," Mia teased, her smile playful.

"Fine. Isang order ng fries para sa lahat!" I declared, making everyone laugh again.

Later that night, habang nasa kwarto ako, I couldn't help but replay the events of the past few days in my head. Winning wasn't really the highlight for me. It was realizing that I wasn't alone. I had a team who believed in me, and together, we pushed through every challenge.

I pulled out my notebook and scribbled a quick note to myself:

"Sometimes, the best victories aren't about winning. They're about learning to trust the people around you and discovering what you're capable of as a team."

For the first time in a long time, I felt proud—not just of myself but of the people I had by my side

Chapter 6: A New Rival

The weeks after the Sophomore Challenge felt calmer, but a certain buzz lingered in the air. San Ignacio High had returned to its usual rhythm—homework, quizzes, and occasional lunch hangouts. But it seemed the Challenge sparked something else, lalo na sa dynamics ng bawat student.

"Have you heard? May bagong transfer student daw sa section ng mga honors," Gabby said one morning as we walked to the cafeteria. "Ang ganda raw, pero sobrang competitive."

"Wow, bagong transfer nanaman?" I asked, curious. "Masyado nang maraming achievers dito, tapos dadagdagan pa nila?"

"Uy, baka naman ma-inspire ka, Jav," Mia teased, her glasses slightly fogged from walking under the sun. "Competition brings out the best in us, sabi nga nila."

"Or it just stresses us out," Carina added, appearing behind us with her usual smirk.

The cafeteria was busier than usual that day. As soon as we stepped inside, a group of students was already crowding around one table.

"Yun siguro yung bagong transfer," Lex said, pointing at the group. "Mukhang big deal ah."

Curious, we walked closer until we caught a glimpse of her. The girl was tall, with sleek hair tied into a ponytail, wearing the honors section uniform. Her confident aura radiated, and she seemed unfazed by the attention.

"Hi, I'm Reina Fernandez," she said in a calm but assertive tone as she introduced herself to some students. "I was the top student at my old school. Hopefully, I can keep that streak here."

"Top student?" Mia whispered beside me. "Mukhang intense siya."

"Reina Fernandez?" Gabby echoed, scratching his head. "Parang familiar. Parang narinig ko na yung name niya dati."

By the time classes resumed, Reina's name was already spreading like wildfire. During Physics, Mrs. Santiago introduced her formally to our class since she would be attending some of our advanced subjects.

"Everyone, this is Reina Fernandez," Mrs. Santiago said. "She'll be joining us for certain sessions, especially for competitive academic activities."

As soon as Reina entered, her gaze landed straight on me.

"So, you're the famous Astorga?" she asked casually, her tone dripping with curiosity.

"Uh, yeah, I guess," I replied, slightly caught off guard.

"I heard your team placed third in the Sophomore Challenge. Not bad," she said with a small smile, though there was something in her tone that felt... challenging.

"Thanks, I guess," I replied, unsure how to respond.

"You might want to keep up, though," she added before taking her seat near the front.

"Okay, what was that?" Gabby whispered from the row behind me.

As the days went by, Reina's presence started to shift the atmosphere. She was confident, skilled, and undeniably smart. During group discussions in Physics, she always had the final say.

Mia, who was usually the class go-to for tough topics, seemed a bit unsettled.

"Okay ka lang?" I asked her after one discussion where Reina completely dominated.

"Yeah, okay naman," she replied, though her voice lacked its usual energy. "She's just... very competitive. Parang ang hirap i-match."

Gabby leaned in. "Don't let her get to you, Mia. Iba ang style mo. Ikaw yung steady at collaborative, siya naman yung medyo soloista."

"Thanks, Gab," Mia said with a faint smile.

One afternoon, as I was walking to the library, I overheard Reina talking to a group of students.

"I don't really see what the fuss is about Javriel Astorga," she said, her voice sharp but calm. "Sure, his team placed in the challenge, but it's not like he's unbeatable."

"Wow, salamat naman sa tiwala," I muttered to myself, shaking my head.

I walked past them, pretending not to care, but her words lingered. It wasn't anger I felt—it was a mix of frustration and determination.

That night, habang nag-aaral ako sa kwarto, I thought about everything. Reina was pushing people, intentionally or not. And in a weird way, maybe that was what I needed.

I grabbed my notebook and wrote a list of things I wanted to improve on—not to compete with her, but to prove something to myself.

"Sometimes, the biggest rival isn't the person challenging you. It's the doubt you carry inside."

Chapter 7: Clash of the Minds

The announcement came during homeroom: San Ignacio High Academic Olympiad—a prestigious inter-school competition known for tough categories ranging from Math to Physics. Naturally, it was the hot topic of the day.

"Okay, listen up, everyone," Mrs. Santiago said, her voice echoing in the classroom. "The Olympiad is only a month away, and I'll be handpicking participants for the team based on academic performance, interest, and dedication. If you're interested, I need you to sign up by the end of the week."

"Jav, sasali ka?" Gabby asked, leaning over his desk.

"Hindi ko pa alam," I replied, tapping my pen against my notebook.

"Alam na. Oo ang sagot," Mia said, looking at me with a knowing smile. "This is your chance to prove na kaya mo, not just for others but for yourself."

"Ikaw ba sasali?" I asked her.

"Of course," she said confidently, though I could see a flicker of hesitation in her eyes.

The week flew by, and when the list of participants was posted on the bulletin board, I wasn't surprised to see

Reina's name at the top. What did surprise me was the number of students who signed up—including Mia, Lex (to everyone's shock), and myself.

Reina's reaction to the list was immediate.

"Well, this should be interesting," she said with a sly smile when she saw my name. "Let's see if you can keep up, Astorga."

The first round of eliminations was a school-wide quiz bee. Twenty students competed, and only five would represent San Ignacio High. The quiz bee was held in the auditorium, and the tension was palpable.

"Breathe, Jav," Mia whispered as we waited for our turn to answer. "Kaya mo 'yan."

"Thanks," I replied, though my heart was pounding.

The questions were brutal. Physics equations, historical dates, literary terms—you name it. But I managed to hold my own, scoring high enough to make it to the top five. Mia and Reina also made the cut, of course.

As the results were announced, Reina walked up to me with a raised eyebrow.

"Not bad," she said, her tone almost playful. "But the real challenge hasn't started yet."

"Looking forward to it," I replied, forcing a confident smile.

The next phase was team selection. Mrs. Santiago divided the top five into two groups: Team Alpha, led by Reina, and Team Beta, led by... me.

"Well, this should be fun," Gabby said, clapping me on the back. He and Mia were both on my team, while Reina's team included Carina and a senior named Daniel, known for his sharp wit.

Team Beta was immediately labeled as the underdog. Reina's reputation alone made her team seem unbeatable.

Practice sessions for the Olympiad were grueling. Mrs. Santiago assigned mock challenges to test teamwork and problem-solving skills. One day, she gave us a particularly tough problem in Physics involving quantum mechanics.

"We've got this," Mia said, her eyes shining with determination. "Jav, analyze the data. Gabby, double-check his calculations. I'll handle the diagrams."

Our teamwork flowed smoothly, and for the first time, I felt like we had a shot.

Meanwhile, rumors were spreading that Reina was taking extra tutoring sessions with some college professors. Her team practiced late into the night, often staying after school.

"Grabe sila," Gabby said one afternoon, watching Reina's group from the gym window. "Parang sila lang ang may karapatan manalo."

"We'll win because we're a team," I said firmly. "Hindi lang dahil magaling ang isa."

The tension between Reina and me reached its peak during a joint practice session. The task was a head-to-head trivia showdown, with questions flying from all subjects.

"Who discovered the photoelectric effect?" Mrs. Santiago asked.

"Albert Einstein," Reina and I answered at the same time.

Our eyes met, and the room seemed to freeze for a moment.

After practice, Mia pulled me aside.

"Jav, alam mo ba bakit competitive masyado si Reina?" she asked quietly.

"No, bakit?" I asked, confused.

"She's trying to prove herself," Mia said. "Gusto niyang ipakita na hindi lang siya magaling academically, but she can lead, too. Sounds familiar, diba?"

I didn't know what to say. Maybe Reina and I weren't so different after all.

The Olympiad was just weeks away, and while the rivalry with Reina burned hotter than ever, something else was growing—respect. I could feel it in the way she looked at me during practices.

But one thing was clear: only one of us would lead San Ignacio High to victory.

Chapter 8: The Final Showdown

The day of the Olympiad arrived, and San Ignacio High's team entered the venue with matching jackets and determined faces. The event was grander than I expected—an enormous auditorium filled with students from different schools, teachers, and even some parents. The stage was set with bright lights, and the air buzzed with tension.

"You ready for this, Jav?" Gabby asked, patting me on the back.

"Ready as I'll ever be," I replied, though my stomach churned with nerves.

Mia adjusted her glasses and gave me a reassuring smile. "We've worked hard for this. Let's show them what Team Beta can do."

On the other side of the hall, Reina and her team were sitting, exuding confidence. She caught my eye and smirked, mouthing, "Bring it on."

The Olympiad was divided into three rounds: a written test, a team challenge, and a final buzzer round. The scores from all rounds would be combined to determine the winner.

Round 1: The Written Test

Each team member had to answer questions individually, with their scores contributing to the team's overall tally. The questions were brutal—everything from advanced Physics equations to obscure world history facts.

I finished with five minutes to spare, but Reina stayed hunched over her paper until the last second.

After the papers were collected, Mia whispered, "Ang intense. Parang hindi ako makahinga the whole time."

"Same," I said, wiping my palms on my pants. "But I think we did okay."

Round 2: The Team Challenge

The second round tested our ability to work together under pressure. Each team was given a complex problem to solve, requiring research, calculations, and a detailed presentation—all within an hour.

"Okay, here's the plan," I said as soon as we received the problem. "Mia, you handle the equations. Gabby, research the background and cross-check the data. I'll focus on structuring the presentation."

Our teamwork was seamless. Mia's calculations were spot-on, Gabby found the perfect examples to support our solution, and we presented confidently.

Reina's team, of course, delivered an impressive presentation as well. Her leadership shone, but their teamwork didn't seem as tight-knit as ours.

Round 3: The Buzzer Round

This was the most nerve-wracking part of the competition. Two teams faced off on stage, answering rapid-fire questions by hitting a buzzer first. The host explained that this round carried the most weight in the final score.

"It's all or nothing," Mia whispered as we took our seats on stage.

The first few questions were straightforward, and both teams scored points. Then came a Physics question that stumped us all.

"What is the Heisenberg Uncertainty Principle?" the host asked.

Reina buzzed in first. "It states that it's impossible to simultaneously determine the exact position and momentum of a particle."

"Correct," the host said, and the audience clapped.

We were tied as the last question loomed. My hands were clammy as I gripped the edge of my seat.

"For the final question: Who proposed the theory of relativity?"

I slammed the buzzer before Reina could. "Albert Einstein!" I blurted out, my voice echoing across the hall.

"Correct!" the host announced, and the crowd erupted into applause.

The Aftermath

When the final scores were tallied, Team Beta emerged victorious by a narrow margin. Gabby threw his arms around me in celebration, and Mia beamed with pride.

"Grabe, Jav! We did it!" Gabby said, his voice full of excitement.

I glanced at Reina, who was clapping politely with a tight smile. Despite her defeat, she approached me after the ceremony.

"Congrats, Astorga," she said, extending her hand.

"Thanks," I replied, shaking her hand firmly. "You were amazing out there."

"You were better today," she admitted, her tone genuine. "But this isn't the last time we'll face each other."

"Looking forward to it," I said, smiling.

As we walked out of the auditorium, the trophy in hand, I felt a sense of accomplishment unlike anything before. Winning wasn't just about beating Reina—it was about proving to myself that I could rise to any challenge.

And for the first time, I realized high school wasn't just about surviving. It was about growing, learning, and finding strength in unexpected places.

After the competition, the bus ride back to San Ignacio was anything but quiet. Gabby couldn't stop reenacting the buzzer round, complete with exaggerated sound effects.

"'Albert Einstein!'" he shouted dramatically, making everyone laugh. "Grabe, Jav, parang ikaw na si Einstein kanina!"

"Hindi naman," I said, shaking my head but unable to hide my smile. "Teamwork lang talaga."

"Uy, oo nga. Pero, Jav, ang bilis ng reflexes mo kanina!" Mia said, adjusting her glasses. "I was so nervous, pero nung ikaw ang sumagot, parang nawala bigla yung kaba ko."

"Honestly, it wasn't just me. Lahat tayo may ginawa. We wouldn't have won without you and Gabby," I replied sincerely.

Pagdating namin sa school, the principal and some teachers were waiting at the entrance to congratulate us. There were cheers and even a small banner that said, "Congratulations, San Ignacio Academic Team!"

"Good job, Team Beta!" Mrs. Santiago said proudly, shaking our hands. "You've made the school proud."

"Thank you, ma'am," I said, feeling a mix of pride and relief.

While the celebration continued, I noticed Reina standing at a distance, talking quietly with her teammates. She glanced in our direction, and for a moment, our eyes met. She gave me a small, almost unnoticeable nod.

It wasn't the loud, confident Reina I was used to seeing. It was something more vulnerable, more real.

The following day, life at San Ignacio returned to normal—well, almost. People in the hallway started calling me "Quiz King," much to Gabby's amusement.

"'Quiz King Astorga'—sarap pakinggan, ano?" he teased.

"Tumigil ka nga," I said, laughing. "Isang competition lang 'yun."

Mia, walking beside us, chuckled. "Deserve mo naman, Jav. Pero... next year, ako naman!"

"Deal," I said, smiling at her determination.

Later that afternoon, Reina approached me while I was studying in the library.

"Hey," she said, pulling out the chair across from me.

"Hey," I replied, surprised.

"Just wanted to say thanks," she began, her voice softer than usual.

"Thanks? Para saan?"

"For pushing me to be better," she admitted. "I've never had someone challenge me like that. You deserved the win."

"Thanks, Reina," I said, genuinely touched. "You were incredible, though. Honestly, I thought you had us."

She smiled faintly. "Next time, maybe I will."

With that, she walked away, leaving me with a new perspective. Reina wasn't just a rival—she was someone who made me better, too.

That night, as I lay in bed staring at the trophy on my desk, I realized the Olympiad wasn't just about winning. It was about growth—mine, Mia's, Gabby's, even Reina's.

It was proof that we were more than just students trying to survive high school. We were individuals capable of rising to any challenge, as long as we worked together and believed in ourselves.

And for the first time in a long while, I felt ready for whatever came next.

Chapter 9: Crossroads of the Heart

"Bakit parang ang hirap ng lahat?" I whispered to myself, sitting on the rooftop of San Ignacio High. The sun was beginning to set, painting the sky in warm shades of orange and pink. I tightened my grip on the railing, feeling the cool metal press against my palms.

The past few days had been overwhelming. My feelings for Mia were no longer a secret, not after what happened at the café. Gabby's confession had thrown everything into chaos. And now, I was left wondering: where do I stand?

I thought back to her words: "I need time to think."

But what if her answer wasn't the one I wanted to hear?

It had been two days since that conversation, and neither Mia nor Gabby had brought it up. Everything felt tense—like a storm waiting to break. Gabby was his usual cheerful self in class, but I could see the way his gaze lingered on Mia. Meanwhile, Mia avoided eye contact with both of us, keeping her head down and focusing on her notes.

After Physics class, Gabby finally cornered me by the lockers.

"Jav, kailangan natin mag-usap," he said, his tone serious.

I nodded. "Alam ko."

We found an empty classroom and sat down, the silence between us heavier than it had ever been.

"Bro," he started, running a hand through his hair. "Alam kong gusto mo rin si Mia."

I nodded again, not trusting myself to speak.

"Pero hindi ko pwedeng basta na lang bitawan yung nararamdaman ko para sa kanya," he continued, his voice trembling slightly. "Matagal ko nang alam na ikaw rin... pero nauna ako, Jav. Alam mo yun."

"Alam ko," I said quietly. "And I respect that, Gabby. Pero hindi ko rin kayang itago yung nararamdaman ko. I care about her, just like you do."

"Hindi ba natin pwedeng ayusin 'to nang hindi nasisira yung pagkakaibigan natin?" he asked, his eyes pleading.

I looked at him, my best friend since day one at San Ignacio, and felt a pang of guilt. "Gusto ko ring ayusin, Gab. Pero paano kung si Mia ang pumili?"

That afternoon, Mia sent us both a message: "Mag-usap tayo sa rooftop after class. Kailangan na natin tapusin 'to."

The hours until that meeting felt like an eternity. When the final bell rang, Gabby and I silently made our way to the rooftop, both of us dreading and anticipating what was to come.

Mia was already there, standing near the edge and staring at the horizon. Her messy hair was tied back, and the light reflected off her glasses, making her expression hard to read.

"Salamat sa pagpunta," she said softly when she saw us.

Gabby and I stood side by side, waiting for her to speak.

"Alam kong mahirap 'to para sa ating tatlo," she began, her voice steady but emotional. "At sa totoo lang, ang hirap din para sa akin."

She looked at Gabby first. "Gab, you've been my best friend for as long as I can remember. Ikaw yung taong nandiyan lagi para sa akin, kahit anong mangyari. You mean so much to me."

Then she turned to me. "Javriel, you came into my life unexpectedly, pero sa maikling panahon, you've made such a big impact. You're kind, smart, and you've always believed in me, kahit minsan hindi ko na kayang maniwala sa sarili ko."

Her voice broke slightly, and she took a deep breath. "Pero kailangan kong maging totoo sa sarili ko. And the truth is... gusto ko si Jav."

The words hung in the air, cutting through the tension like a knife. Gabby's shoulders slumped, and he let out a shaky breath.

"I'm sorry, Gabby," Mia said, tears in her eyes. "I didn't mean to hurt you. You're still my best friend, and I hope someday you can forgive me."

Gabby nodded slowly, wiping his face with the back of his hand. "Okay lang, Mia. I just want you to be happy."

As Gabby left the rooftop, I felt a mix of relief and guilt. I looked at Mia, who was staring down at her feet, and took a step closer.

"Mia," I said softly, "sigurado ka ba? Ayokong pilitin ka o bigyan ka ng pressure."

She looked up at me, her eyes shining. "Sigurado ako, Jav. Matagal ko nang nararamdaman 'to, pero natakot lang akong sabihin. Ngayon lang ako naging handa."

For the first time in days, I smiled—a real, genuine smile. "Salamat," I said, my voice barely above a whisper.

She smiled back, and in that moment, the weight of the past few days seemed to disappear.

As the sun dipped below the horizon, painting the sky in deep purples and blues, I realized something.

Sometimes, love isn't about winning or losing. It's about finding the courage to be honest—with yourself, and with the people you care about.

And for the first time, I felt like everything was going to be okay.

Chapter 10: Twists of Fate

The following weeks after the rooftop confession felt like a dream, yet not without its challenges. Mia and I grew closer, but Gabby's absence in our dynamic created a hollow space. He stopped hanging out with us entirely, excusing himself with basketball practices and "other things."

One afternoon, Mia and I sat in our usual spot at the library. She was flipping through her notes, but her face was etched with guilt.

"Jav," she started, her voice soft. "Napapansin mo ba si Gabby? Hindi pa rin siya okay."

I nodded, sighing. "Alam ko. He's my best friend, Mia. Kaya nga ang hirap nitong lahat."

Mia hesitated. "Do you think we did the right thing?"

Her question caught me off guard, but I held her gaze. "Mia, hindi ko rin alam kung tama lahat ng 'to. Pero ang alam ko lang, totoo yung nararamdaman ko para sa'yo."

She smiled faintly but didn't look entirely convinced.

The tension came to a head during the school's annual Acquaintance Night. Gabby was there, but he kept his distance, opting to stick with his basketball teammates. Mia and I tried to enjoy the evening, but the weight of unspoken words lingered between us and Gabby.

As the night wore on, Reina—a mutual friend—pulled Mia aside. I watched them talk from across the room, wondering what was so urgent. Mia returned, her face pale.

"Jav, kailangan natin mag-usap," she said, pulling me toward an empty hallway.

"What's wrong?" I asked, concerned.

"Reina told me something... something about Gabby."

My chest tightened. "Ano?"

She hesitated, her eyes searching mine. "She overheard Gabby talking to someone. He said he's transferring schools next semester."

The words hit me like a punch to the gut. "What? Bakit?!"

"I don't know," she said, her voice cracking. "But I think... it's because of us."

The next day, I confronted Gabby at the gym after practice. He was sitting on the bleachers, towel draped over his shoulders, looking exhausted.

"Gab," I said, my voice firm. "Totoo ba 'to? You're transferring?"

He looked at me, surprised, but then his expression hardened. "Sinabi ni Reina, 'no?"

I nodded. "Gab, ano 'to? Bakit ka aalis?"

He scoffed, standing up and throwing his towel on the bench. "Alam mo na ang sagot, Jav. Hindi ko kayang magpanggap na okay lang. Every time I see you and Mia together, parang tinutusok yung dibdib ko."

"Bro," I said, my voice breaking. "I never wanted this to happen. Ayokong masira yung pagkakaibigan natin."

"Well, guess what? Sira na," he snapped.

His words cut deep, and for a moment, I didn't know what to say.

"Gab, please," I pleaded. "Huwag mong talikuran 'to. You're more than just this. Ang dami mong kayang gawin, and running away won't fix anything."

He looked at me, his eyes filled with pain. "Alam ko. Pero hindi rin madaling kalimutan yung nararamdaman ko. Kaya kung gusto mong tulungan ako... give me space, Jav. For now."

I nodded reluctantly, my heart heavy. "I'll respect that, Gab. Pero tandaan mo, andito pa rin ako. Hindi magbabago 'yon."

A week later, during an ordinary lunch break, a commotion erupted in the cafeteria. Reina came rushing to our table, her face flushed with panic.

"Mia! Jav! Si Gabby—nag-collapse siya sa gym!"

We bolted out of our seats and sprinted to the gym, our hearts racing. When we got there, Gabby was lying on the floor, pale and unconscious, surrounded by his teammates.

"What happened?!" I demanded, kneeling beside him.

"Di pa siya kumakain kanina," one of the players said. "Ang tigas ng ulo, ayaw magpahinga!"

Mia was already calling for the school nurse while I stayed by Gabby's side, gripping his hand tightly.

"Gab, wake up," I whispered. "Bro, kailangan ka namin."

Gabby recovered after a few hours in the infirmary, but the incident served as a wake-up call for all of us. That evening, Mia and I visited him at his house, carrying his favorite food as a peace offering.

"Ang kulit mo, ah," Mia scolded gently, setting the food on his desk. "Kung hindi ka pa natumba, hindi mo pa aaminin na hindi ka okay."

Gabby laughed weakly. "Sorry na."

We spent hours talking, laughing, and finally addressing the tension that had been building for weeks. Gabby admitted that transferring schools had been a knee-jerk reaction and that collapsing in the gym had forced him to rethink his choices.

"Alam ko na hindi ko kayo pwedeng sisihin," he said, looking at both of us. "Kailangan ko lang tanggapin na minsan, hindi talaga para sa'yo yung taong gusto mo."

As we walked home that night, Mia slipped her hand into mine.

"Ang dami nating pinagdaanan," she said softly.

I nodded, squeezing her hand. "Pero at least ngayon, maayos na. Kahit papaano."

She smiled up at me, her eyes shining. "Salamat, Jav. For everything."

As we walked under the streetlights, I realized that while love could be messy and complicated, it was also worth fighting for.

And with Mia by my side, I knew we could face anything together.

The days following Gabby's recovery were quieter but significantly lighter. There was an unspoken truce between the three of us. While things weren't entirely back to normal, there was progress—a foundation to rebuild what had been broken.

One afternoon, as Mia and I walked out of the library, we bumped into Gabby on the way to the court.

"Hey," he greeted, adjusting his gym bag. His tone was casual, but his smile held a trace of sincerity that hadn't been there before.

"Hi, Gab," Mia replied, her voice tentative.

He shifted his weight, looking at me. "Jav, we're short one for basketball practice. Libre ka ba?"

The question caught me off guard. It was the first olive branch Gabby had extended since everything happened.

"Uh, sure," I said, glancing at Mia. She smiled and gave me a small nod.

"I'll wait for you here," she offered. "Kaya mo 'yan."

At the court, the tension from before was gone. Gabby didn't treat me differently, even cracking jokes between plays. It was like old times—almost.

As the practice ended, Gabby patted me on the back. "Thanks for filling in, bro."

"No problem," I replied, wiping sweat off my forehead.

He hesitated before speaking again. "Jav... alam ko na hindi madali 'to para sa ating lahat. Pero gusto kong malaman mo na sinusubukan ko. For you, for Mia. For us."

I nodded, my chest tightening. "Same here, Gab. Alam kong matagal bago talaga maging okay, pero andito ako. Hindi kita iiwan."

For the first time in weeks, he smiled genuinely. "Okay, deal. Pero bawal kayong PDA sa harap ko."

I laughed. "Noted."

When I returned to Mia, she was waiting under the large acacia tree near the court. The sun was setting again, casting a golden glow around her. She looked up from her book and smiled when she saw me.

"Kamusta kayo ni Gabby?" she asked, closing her book.

"Better," I said, sitting beside her. "It's not perfect, but we're getting there."

She leaned her head on my shoulder, letting out a small sigh. "I'm glad. Ayoko ng may nasasaktan."

I wrapped an arm around her, pulling her closer. "We'll figure it out, Mia. Together."

That night, as I lay in bed, I replayed the events of the past few weeks in my mind. It had been a whirlwind—emotions running high, relationships tested, and hearts put on the line. But through it all, one thing had become clear:

Mia wasn't just someone I liked. She was someone I cared about deeply—someone I was willing to fight for.

And for the first time in a long time, I felt like I was exactly where I was meant to be.

About the Author

Jariv - Reuel Josh V. Anda

Reuel Josh a young and passionate teenager he loves reading books that is related to him, he loves his parents. he always think about them.

www.ingramcontent.com/pod-product-compliance
Lightning Source LLC
LaVergne TN
LVHW041636070526
838199LV00052B/3387